$T°$

KINESIOPHOBIA
a novel

Meghan S. Guidry

$T°$

THERA BOOKS
Sacramento, California
SAY / SOMETHING

Kinesiophobia: A Novel
Copyright © 2022 by Meghan S. Guidry

Cover artwork by Dawn Baja

Author photograph by Meghan S. Guidry

Cover design by Mona Z. Kraculdy

ISBN: 979-8-9863098-1-1
Library of Congress Control Number: 2022948655

A Thera Books First Edition, November 2022

Printed in the United States of America

*For Louis Allen Guidry
and everyone else
who carries the wires.*

ON THE ORIGINS OF DROWNING

They crossed the ocean nearly 400 years ago. Loaded a great
gray ark with livestock and supplies. Starcharts and wine.
Promises of glory dripped from their tongues. Prayer cards
tucked by their breasts to bless crossing the Atlantic from
France to a new world calling colonizers like a siren.

On departure day they laughed as mooring ropes went slack.
Laughed as they emptied a barrel of wine. Laughed as the
steeples disappeared on the horizon and the sea swallowed
them whole.

They sailed west. Cut the curve of the ocean. Their wake
a wound on its surface. The waves churned blue and gray.
Storms spiraled like spiders. The ark heaved in the swells.
They shifted sails and spat miasma into the sea. Hurled
insults at the water as if that could keep their drowning at
bay.

The journey wore them to starvation frames. Disease tore

through the bow. They tipped their dead over the deck. Drank to the departed. Drained their wine and threw the waste to the waves.

That was how the Atlantic got a taste of this bloodline fleeing France. Their bodies moonglow smooth, slipping beneath the brine. Their lungs like cathedrals the ocean could occupy.

They felt the water begin to watch them. The sound of its swells like hunger. They kept their days on deck. Told stories about the land that awaited them. Covered the sound of the waves with music and wine.

But at night they could feel it. The ocean slamming against the ark. The ocean in their skulls mapping cracks into the belly of the boat. Mapping paths down their throats. They crossed and crossed themselves again. Pressed prayer cards to their breasts. Repeated *land* like a benediction they could will into existence.

They cheered the day they saw the shore in the west. Shouted curses at the waves. Drank their wine. Called themselves safe.

But the ocean had traced them through every mouthful of miasma they spat. Every gash across its surface in their wake. Every body they tipped over the rails. The water knew them by taste. And would never forget their scents.

They anchored in the harbor. Thin slips pulled them safe ashore. They stared at their ark and the Atlantic behind it, and vowed to never cross again.

They became a beacon others would follow. A line like a wire from homeland to granite shores. They endured bitter winter famines and snow white as sails. Still, they clung to land and maintained their vow. *Whatever our fate, anything is better than facing the ocean again.*

They thought they would be safe on land. But they didn't know what they'd set in motion: the wires and the wolves, the copper cross, the dead in boxes above the ground, the city underwater, the miasma in our throats?

They didn't know they would become the origin of countless generations of this family the Atlantic would claim. That everyone thereafter would drown in their place. That we would never run, even when we saw the waves.

Ever since their crossing, everyone in my family gets marked by the Atlantic and stalked by its waters. Everyone gets a wire buried in their bodies that becomes a beacon for the brine. Everyone's lungs are one mistake away from filling with the ocean.

My family is destined to drown. All I can do is scream *how dare you cross the ocean.* Your ark that split the Atlantic in two. Because of you, Acadia was dragged to the bottom of the sea. Because of you, the levees broke and buried New Orleans. Because of you, the hospital filled with water and my father died in my arms.

I want to understand how we got here. How we became a sacrifice to the sea. How my family saw tragedy on the horizon time and time again and never ran. How that paralysis became our inheritance. How the ocean would never lose our scents or stop trying to pull us underwater.

What I've learned is this started centuries ago with a crossing
the Atlantic still hasn't forgotten. With a boat like an ark
that sailed across the sea, carrying my ancestors who thought
the danger was in the passage and not what comes after.

ACADIA

WE BROKE LENT FOR SEVEN YEARS

There was no church in Pointe Prime when Girrard arrived. Seven years since the priest's separation from his flock. Seven years since the British demanded oaths Acadia wouldn't sign. Seven years since they were forced from their homes and tracked east, closer to the great gray ocean.

Seven years brought Girrard back to the colony. To the new village they built. An impossible reassembly. Reunion like communion safely under tongue.

Noël was first to greet him. To lead the priest through the village. He explained that the British blockade had brought starvation to their shores. Their men were turning into ghosts. New mothers were too frail to prime their milk. Children curled like ferns in fire ash, too weak to survive the nights. It fell to Noël to divide supplies. The awful arithmetic of who would survive.

Noël paused. Smiled at his friend. Shook his hands. *Despite what they'd endured, surely God must be good to guide their priest's return.*

So Girrard seeded cathedrals in kitchens. Provided last rites in cooking ash. Learned the lore the colony carried to this new shore. That crimson clouds spelled shellfish in the shallows. That they could see yellow eyes in the birches at night. That they felt uneasy close to the ocean. As if it knew them from long before. As if it was waiting for the chance to drag them back.

Winter came and depleted their supplies. Brought Lent closer to their lips. Girrard watched women pluck periwinkles from the rocks. Stretch dandelion greens into broth. Clutch copper rings they carried like rosaries. Like food and fire. Like there was something more they could give up.

When the dark dawn of Ash Wednesday arrived, Girrard wrote his sermon. Went outside to the commons. Braced his Bible with shells smooth as moonrise. He called the colony there. He said God saw they had nothing to relinquish this season. Saw their piety and plight. The Lord loved them, and wouldn't suffer them to spread starvation like contagion through their ranks.

So the colony broke Lent that year. Survived. Sustained by his sermon. In spring, they built a church. Fell pine for corner posts. Tore wood from boats. Collected all the copper they carried and laid it in a mold.

The whole colony watched as they melted the metal. Watched molten strands stretch as they stirred. The forge threw shadows thin as wires across their bodies. Black lines over collarbones and wrists. The shadows crossed their bodies, flashed metallic on their skin, then disappeared.

When it was done, the metal set like waves. Became a copper cross they hung in the church above a window overlooking the water. To thank God for winter's survival. To thank Girrard for his return. To remind them of the drowning circling their lungs and hold the ocean at bay.

HIS THROAT BECAME A COASTLINE

Six years after the priest's return, Girrard had learned to count the days like rosaries. He fell trees and stripped the trunks. Pulled purslane from the ground. Gathered pine for evening fires. Blue smoke that burned his eyes and blurred the ocean.

The colony had grown more fearful of the sea since he arrived. He watched children run too fast toward the shore, stop short, and clutch wrists or rub their jaws. As if something in their bodies flared near the water and was begging them back to land.

Whispers ran through the village that summer. The colony came to Girrard one by one. They said the British blockade was never coming down. That they meant to starve Acadia into submission. Into bodies too weak to resist. Into boats that would disappear over the horizon.

The priest swallowed their fears. Felt them turn solid in his throat. He could only nod and give them assurances. Give them scriptures and promises of grace. Give children hymns to guard their dreams from drowning.

He wrote letters begging mercy and sermons late into the night. The ocean was always churning outside. He couldn't ignore how the waves curled like a mouth. How they surged in his skull when he tried to sleep. How something stung his palm every time he went near the water. How the cross had tarnished and turned half copper, half drowning green.

He traced his fingers down the cross. Repeated that it was just their fear. Superstition fueled by starvation. Lore like wires strung through years. Surely God would save them. Ease the blockade. Fill their starving frames and uphold the coast between Acadia and the Atlantic.

Girrard stared out the window behind the altar. The ocean spilled behind blue smoke. It was always swallowing the moonlight. Always seething at the shore. He felt something sharp pierce his palm and glanced at his hand. There was nothing there. But the colony's pleas were crowding in his throat. Staring at the coast. Begging him to run.

He tried to swallow like he could pull their words back into his body. Like he could hold their pleas to keep the ocean at bay. Like his hand wasn't burning and the word run wasn't turning solid in his throat.

He had to talk to Noël. Bring their concerns to bear. Explain that he knew there were rumors. Knew the superstitions the colony carried. And confess that maybe those upheld the coastline that divided them from drowning.

The burning in his palm stopped with that thought. The ocean ebbed from his skull back to the black mass of water. He sat on the sanctuary floor. Whispered the hymns he taught children to guard their dreams. To quiet the waves. To forget the tide pulling them toward the coastline and the moonlight the ocean always swallowed whole.

THE WOLF IN THE WHEEL WELLS

Autumn bore warnings through the blockade. The British had plans to cut the colony from the coast. Lay siege to everyone still clinging to the shore. Parse them into arks. Send them back across that ocean, dark as drowning.

The colony begged their priest to intercede. The British would put them on boats where the Atlantic would claim them. They winced when they said the ocean's name. Rubbed jawlines and legs. The pain in Girrard's hand burned like a wire piercing his skin. But there was never a wound. Only lines in his palm like the trajectories across the sea.

He went to Noël. The word run like a stone in his throat. He told his friend the rumors. The fears. That this was an exodus, anew. That masts would come bearing starvation sails and the colony would be crushed under their weight. They had to go before the British brought them back to the ocean.

Noël lowered his head and asked Girrard if he remembered their old village. The year the locusts descended on the harvest and blight shriveled the grain. Famine and bitter winters. Families curled around the hearth drinking dying ember heat. Howls from the treeline. Shadows and all the wolves therein.

Someone always died those nights. In the morning, Noël would test the earth with his spade. The ground would never open. So Noël and Girrard wrapped the dead. Placed them on a cart. Rode away from the village. Drove to distant clearings. Laid the body on the ground. Made mounds of stones. Prayed aloud. Their words visible in winter air as wolfsong wove through the treeline.

They rode back in twilight. Noël drove the cart. Girard watched the wheels glide over the earth, solid as the bodies it wouldn't claim. He watched the shadows in the axles, dark as treelines. Howls spilled behind them. Only the stones stood between their dead, the beasts, and the desecration that comes after.

Noël faced his friend and shook his head. They'd survived much worse before. Endured. They wouldn't run on rumors. On fears of masts. On the belief that the ocean wanted them back.

Noël winced as he spoke. Reached to rub the back of his neck. Then dropped his hand to Girrard's shoulder. He repeated that the colony would need their priest to survive another winter. To brave ungiving ground. To face treelines spilling wolfsong anew.

Girrard nodded. Gave his word. The vow curved over the mass in his throat. Over the pain in his hand. Over the colony's pleas. Like they could pile stones to keep the beasts at bay. Like the ground wouldn't refuse them. Like yellow eyes weren't waiting between the birch and empty hulls weren't on the other side of the horizon.

THE MOURNING SHORE

The masts appeared in October. White sails against the sea. The ships moored in the harbor. Spilled thin slips into the shallows. The colony seized on the shore. Women's hands over children's mouths to keep the water from their lungs.

Noël stood sentry as the British soldiers disembarked. Officers with proclamations in their hands cut through colony lines. Division drip from their lips.

Noël led the officers to his home. Girrard followed behind. The door was closed when he arrived. But he could hear their voices diagramming an expulsion. The flint of familiar names. The piercing in his hand. *Run* lodged in his throat. The ocean folding over their heads.

When it was done, Noël gathered the colony-. Told them they were being sent back to France. Three arks would bear them: Ruby, Duke Williams, and Violet. But they would be together. He'd spent the day rearranging names to keep their families whole. To keep bloodlines close the moment the ocean opened before them.

The colony wailed all through the night as they parsed their lives apart. Women held half-moons beneath red eyes. Filled faded fabric squares with what they couldn't leave behind. Seeds and pocket knives. Lullabies tucked under children's tongues. Herbs like prayer cards by their breasts. Anything they could cling to in the water.

Acadia was forced to the shore the next morning. The architects called their names. Packed them tight into slips and ferried them to the arks. Girrard watched them disappear. Clutched the copper cross he'd saved. Prayed for safety. Prayed for every departure. Prayed the pain burning in his body was wrong.

Girrard, Noël, and his family were last. The men watched Noël's wife and children disappear into the Duke Williams. Captain Nichols waited beside them. His duty, he explained, was to ensure the colony was clear. That every name was packed into its ark. That no one would be left behind. They stood in silence until the slip returned and Nichols motioned for them to enter.

They were the last to leave Pointe Prime. The last to lift their soles from shore. Feel mussel shells underfoot. Breathe sticky pine into their lungs. The architects pushed the slip into the water and began to row.

Girrard looked back at the land. The pain in his palm flared.

The priest held his hand to home. And as twilight covered
the shore, the coastline disappeared through his fingers until
he could almost see yellow eyes opening in the birches and
wolfsong curling through the trees.

THE STARVING ARK

The arks cut across the Atlantic for a month, then more. The colony confined to the hold. The horizon tightened like a wire. The priest ferried prayers from belly to deck. At night he slept clutching the cross. The copper burned between his palms. The ocean indigo with anticipation.

Girrard heard the distant crack of wood one evening. He raced to the deck. Saw the Violet slipping into the sea. The screams. The priest held the cross. Tried to remember the ledger. All the names in the belly of the ark like wooden walls were enough to save them from the ocean.

He stayed on deck all night as the Violet sank. Held the cross toward the disappearing mast. Last rites for the colony divided. Half copper. Half drowning green.

Nichols pushed them onward, east then south through December winds. The deck iced in silver scales. Architects screamed orders in the gusts. Nichols strained for signs of safe passage. Girrard mouthed benedictions to the waves.

The Duke Williams lurched one day in early dawn. A crack like thunder from the hull. Girrard wrapped his hands around the rail. Nichols and Noël raced below. Girrard ran to the hold where the colony was confined. Children curled and shook on their parents' laps. Something flickered in the curves of their spines. Glowed in fists wrapped around rosaries. Glinted in their eyes. Like accusations that he could have saved them.

Girrard climbed back to deck. Noël motioned for the priest. Explained there had been a breach. The ocean was pouring in. Architects and Acadia alike would have to pump the water to keep the ark afloat. Their only chance to keep from drowning.

They began to push the Atlantic back. Parse the ocean into buckets and drop it from the deck. Noël led the pumps. Girrard carried the cross through the ark offering solace over the piercing pain in his hand. Over the waves and their hunger slamming into the ark. Over the word *run* seized like a tumor in his throat.

He returned to Noël to offer prayer. Sweat ran like rain down his friend's body as he manned the pumps. But as the priest began to speak, he saw it. Something in Noël's neck. Visible through his skin. Stretched and gleaming. A strand like a wire. Like when they forged the cross. Like those shadows of molten metal put copper in their bodies. Like the glow he'd seen in the colony cowering in the hold.

Girrard checked his palm. Saw the copper stretched beneath his skin, palm to wrist. Followed by the ocean tracking a crossing they carried in their bodies. Tracking the inheritance that was coming to claim them.

MOONRISE OVER MIASMA

They pumped for days. Forced water back to sea. Divided
their drowning in delays. But the ocean always returned.
Always climbed higher. Drawn by the air in their lungs.
Drawn by bodies it knew by taste. Drawn by the wires
beaming beneath their skin.

Nichols tried to reach another ship in the distance. He took
a slip and sailed toward salvation. When he returned, they
watched the boat glide past them. Sails disappearing down
the horizon. The sun dropping west. The ocean rising toward
their feet. Nichols disappeared with Noël. Girrard stayed on
deck. The cross in his hands. The wire burning in his palm.

When they returned, Noël hung his head. The copper
flashed in his neck. Nichols assembled Acadia on the deck.
He said noble Noël had spoken with the voice of the whole
colony. Agreed the slips could only hold a few. Agreed only

the architects could navigate the sea to safety. Agreed that they should go. Acadia would stay.

The colony screamed. They tore their hair. Grabbed their wrists. The wires burning. The ocean pouring in. Girrard clutched the cross. Noël stood alone. His shadow on the deck, distorted and stretched. Like a monster. Like their deaths. Like the darkness holding winter wolves they braved so long ago.

The ark began to angle. The architects packed their slips. Kicked women tearing at their clothes. Spat at crying children. Acadia grasped at Girrard for release. From the copper burning in their bodies. From the ocean clawing at their breasts.

The ark heaved. Angled steeper toward the sea. The slips lowered the architects to safety. Nichols waited in the last open boat. The last empty seats. Noël moved toward the priest, and pressed Girrard toward escape. Toward some arrangement made. Toward God hoarded by the living and last rites delivered across the waves.

Girrard clutched the rails. Noël shook his head. Pushed the priest onto the boat. The colony cried behind him. The moon clawed higher. Nichols gave the order to lower. The ropes went slack. Noël alone. Acadia aflame. Girrard reached out his hand. Held the cross over the deck. Noël took it. Pressed it to his chest. Something darkened in Noël's shadow stretched on the deck. The shape skewed to beast. Knees bent back. Two glints flashed yellow like moonrise over black ocean.

Nichols lowered the slip to the water. Girrard tried to speak last rites but the words turned solid in his throat.

A sound rose from the ark as they sailed away. Noël's voice leading hymns through the screams. The ocean at their feet, their knees. Girrard's rites across the waves. The ocean at their waists. Every wire growing bright. Reflecting copper on the water. The ocean black and spiraling. A mouth swallowing the wails. Their voices slipping one by one into the Atlantic. Until it was quiet. Until it was full. Until every gleam of copper disappeared into miasma like the massacre never happened.

Nichols told his men to row. Girrard screamed and gripped his wrist. The wire burned in his arm. Then he heard a crack from where the ocean swallowed the ark. Like the hull was breaking again. Like wood and thunder and rage. A howl cut across the waves. The priest turned around. But there was nothing other than the ocean and moonglow covering the grave.

IN BEDS MARKED FOR BURNING

The slips cut west until they reached land. Nichols found an inn. Arranged for them to stay. Put Girrard in the back and forced him to write the benedictions that delivered them from drowning.

That night, the architects drank. Nichols raised his glass, proclaimed a toast to honor brave Acadia. The colony, he said, that told them they must go and cheered their departure as the boats lowered into the water. *No tears. No begging. Truly they are each in heaven.*

Girrard sat beside him. The wire burning murder. The colony in tears. The colony clawing at his sleeves. The colony on their knees. Drawn straight into the ocean's waiting mouth. He tried to speak. The words seized solid in his throat. Ocean and murder and run. So he turned away. Faced the far wall. Watched the architects' shadows grow black in the firelight.

He saw something churn in Nichols' shadow. Darker than drowning. A beast larger than a man took form. Stretched across the floor. Its claws like scythes. Back-bent knees. A Wolf with blazing yellow eyes. It looked at Girrard and growled before it disappeared.

He began to see it everywhere. In shadows draped over fireplaces. In shadows under tables where the architects rewrote the sinking of the ark. In shadows above Nichols' bed while he slept. Fire eyes and wolfsong. The howl as Acadia drowned.

The priest stopped sleeping. Laid awake. Locked eyes with the Wolf that seemed to blink from shadow to shadow. Snarled at the architects asleep on their beds. As if it could sense who sank the ark. As if it knew the wires burning on the deck. The wires on the ocean floor. The colony a beacon beaming copper under black water.

Night after night, Girard watched the beast. Watched it hover in the dark above the architects like a wave. Like rage. Like it wanted to set their beds on fire. Burn Nichols in his sleep. Burn the inn. Erase the bodies that justified this slaughter.

The Wolf growled. Blinked to curtain shadows. Girrard clenched his hands and met its eyes. A communion of wounds. The fire couldn't pull them from the brine. Couldn't change that other colonies bore the wires. That Acadia was destined for drowning.

The priest stared at the beast. Knew the Wolf could sense the other wires. Could sense the ocean and its hunger. Could sense the crossing from generations before that led the Atlantic to them.

He realized that the Wolf couldn't move. It could only blink shadow to shadow. Bound to everyone with copper in their bodies. Paralyzed by all the times they didn't run.

But the Wolf would be dragged everywhere the wires went. A witness to all their drownings. Destined to track every massacre thereafter.

Girrard stumbled from his bed. Lit the candle on his desk. Took paper and ink. Wrote two lines for Acadia. For his friends. For his failure to run. For the work the Wolf would inherit. A plea to sever the ocean from their scents. A prayer for the drowned and all the drowning coming after.

Blessed is the beast who finds the wires
and pulls us safe ashore.

KATRINA

WE BROKE LENT FOR SEVEN YEARS

My father took me to New Orleans every year to visit his family. A world of parishes and parades. A wire between our life in Boston and the impossible city beneath the sea.

Centuries before, the Acadians pooled in Louisiana. The survivors of a thousand exiles. They brought memories of arks and white sails. They brought copper wires in their bodies and passed them onto new generations. They learned to cut channels in the earth. Reroute the water. Bury their dead above ground. They sewed the surnames of those who disappeared in the ocean onto their own. Carried them like hymnals beneath their tongues so the drowned could live beyond the brine.

And they brought the Wolf. The creature tied to their nexus of wires. Snarling at the coast and something hungry beyond the horizon.

They caught glimpses of the beast with yellow eyes and back-bent knees in their shadows. Heard howls winding through the cypress. Felt it watching from marshes where the ocean encroached. They named it Rougarou and scared children into keeping tradition by saying it would rip out their throats if they broke Lent for seven years.

New Orleans grew on ground suffused with this story. The wires and the Wolf became lore as they cut the city into parishes. Dug channels down the streets. Erected levees to keep the ocean at bay. Placed plaster statues of saints with half-moon eyes in cemeteries of great stone boxes guarding the dead.

My father grew up in New Orleans. Grew up where magnolias summoned Mardi Gras and all the starvation that follows. Grew up with his grandmother whispering stories about wires and arks. About a monster in the dark that would find him if he didn't fast. He always laughed. The Wolf was always frozen outside under the azaleas. Growing dimmer by the generation.

My father left when he was twenty-one. Went to Boston for law school. A new world without wires and wolves. That first year, he hid in the library. Practiced away his accent. Repeated *your honor* crisp and cool. Every annunciation made something burn behind his knee. The pain stretched like a wire. The copper calling him home.

He settled in Boston and stopped observing Lent. He never mentioned Acadia or the arks. Never told me about the Wolf in the shadows. Never believed we had wires in our bodies. But he always brought me back.

   MEGHAN S. GUIDRY

Every year, we boarded a plane to return to New Orleans. Every year, the wires summoned us home. Every year we flew south along a flightpath gleaming miles above the ocean that had never lost our scents.

HIS THROAT BECAME A COASTLINE

My father noticed the storm before it was named. An image on the news of a white spiral like a spider curling in the Gulf. He called his brother to check. My uncle teased him for being up north too long. *These things usually spin out over the ocean. Nothing to do but watch and wait.*

We watched the storm spin heavy. Draw something deep from the Atlantic. My father clenched his jaw while the newscasts blared. During commercials, he repeated what he knew about the levees: a network of palms to press the ocean back. A thousand traps to catch the waves. A way to save the living and the dead from being swallowed by the brine.

When we visited New Orleans, my father always brought me to the cemeteries. Iron gates. Stone tombs atop the earth. He explained that if the city flooded, the earth would soften and push the coffins back. So the dead were placed in boxes

   MEGHAN S. GUIDRY

above the ground. Burials on land below the level of the sea. As if we'd never left the ark.

We watched the news for days. The name of the storm started spilling from every anchor's mouth. Katrina scratched their throats. My father fixated on the news. Storm models overlaid his city. Memories shaped like hurricanes. Arms spiraled over familiar streets. Cathedrals and feasts. Saints' days and canals. Lakeshores where he and his brother kicked crawfish mounds until crimson claws emerged from the mud.

My father called his brother the night they named the storm. The night they tracked its path straight toward the city. I listened from the kitchen as they talked. Their conversation halved by the phone. Questions about evacuations and how many days they had before landfall. My father tensed at answers I couldn't hear. He muted the news and disappeared upstairs.

I went into the living room. Watched the anchors mouth Katrina. I thought I could see blades in their throats. Thought I could see something darken in a shadow on the screen. Thought the map of the ocean was turning deeper blue like every broadcast was angled toward drowning.

I felt something flare in my hips. The television flashed to live footage of the ocean. Gray waves clawed the coastline. Dragged themselves toward the screen as if they could break the glass.

My father came back downstairs. Put the phone on its cradle. Unmuted the news. The picture clicked back to to a map. The storm over the gulf. The living room flooded blue. White spirals climbed the walls. My father said the levees would protect them. But he clenched his jaw as Katrina spilled from anchors' mouths. From storm models bearing its name. From the ocean's design on our family trapped hundreds of miles away.

THE WOLF IN THE WHEEL WELLS

We kept the news on constantly. The storm suffused our house. Blue light on white walls. We watched the updates like the diagnosis would change. As if we could shift the track. As if the Atlantic wasn't on the other side of that screen.

My father called his brother with every development. Preparations. Evacuations. He asked my uncle about their plans. Begged him to come stay with us. His voice refracted through endless questions. A thousand words to avoid saying one. *Run.*

I sat beside him on the couch as they talked. Muted the television. The newscast cut to scenes of people flooding stores for supplies. Nailing pressboard to windows. Packing belongings into cars. The cargo a gridwork to salvage something of home.

Every car on the screen blazed under sunlight. Under the weight of what they could save. I stared at the screen. At the shadows that wrung the wheels. At something even darker in the circumference.

My father began to pace. Still on the phone. Walking the length of the living room until he disappeared into the kitchen. I watched him leave, then looked back at the TV. I noticed something beading at the border of the television. Pooling in the corner of the screen. Seeping into the room.

Something began burning in my hips. Thin lines running sacrum to knees. The news jumped from cars to storm maps. I twisted my legs to try and quiet the pain. To try and forget the conversation. Forget those cars and the boxes stacked like graves. Forget those sections of shadow darker than the rest.

But something was watching their escape as they drove away from the ocean. As the storm drummed beneath their shoulder blades. As if anything could stop the erasure. As if the Atlantic wouldn't find a way. As if there weren't wires strung between our bodies and the drowning we inherited.

My legs burned. I tried to focus on the screen. The storm spinning over the sea. The water fading teal to blue to black. There was something in the shadows of those cars tracking this new exodus. Pushing them away from the ocean that would swallow them whole. I stared at the TV and saw yellow eyes flicker in a shadow. I tensed, and averted my gaze. When I looked back it was still there. Still staring into the room. I looked at the television, at the corner where something was seeping through. I looked at the yellow locked in that shadow and mouthed the word *run*.

The eyes disappeared. The pain in my hips broke. My legs went cold. Like they were submerged. Like the ocean was always an injury away.

My father was still on the phone. I could hear his voice from the kitchen. I stared at the screen. At the shadows and the eyes they once contained. At the edge where something was bleeding through. I walked to the television, traced my fingers down to the corner, and looked at my hand. Water on my fingertips. The familiar smell of brine. The ocean moving through the screen. I wiped it off with my sleeve and watched another bead form in the corner.

My father came back into the living room and hung up the phone. Unmuted the television. It flashed to an image of the dome. Blinding bronze. An announcement that they would open its doors so people could ride out the storm.

My hips throbbed again. Numbers for city hotlines slashed the screen. They blurred the corner where I'd wiped the water off. And I could see the image of the dome where the survivors would be packed. Trapped with something already waiting in the gridwork of this new ark.

MOURNING SHORE

My father made parallel preparations for the storm. Moved books and notepads to the living room. Blankets to the couch that would become his bed. I brewed coffee to keep us awake and wiped away the ocean seeping through the screen.

We sat in silence. The news in overdrive. Interviews and projected paths. Helicopters circling the city like vultures, feeding on images of before. My father said the names of every sight he recognized like a benediction and an anagram of goodbye.

Engineers were interviewed to explain the levees. Their networks of locks and walls stretched like wires around the city. My father drank the science like medicine. Like a sign. Like the time the ocean lunged and swallowed Acadia in a mouthful of arks.

The newscast lurched to breaking scenes. Live outside the dome. Bronze curves like a shore. The roof white as sails. Thousands of people. The coming waves. The graves atop the ground to engineer the ocean away from the dead.

My father lit a cigar. White smoke spiraled up the walls. Water beaded at the corner of the screen. The ocean riding wires into the room. Into in the air. Pooling at our mouths. Mapping down our throats. The word *run* repeating in my head like a hymn.

Onscreen, people arranged their belongings on sidewalk squares. Eyes wet with coming waves. Reporters shoved microphones toward their mouths. *What made you come? What did you bring? And what did you leave behind?*

A bead of the Atlantic dripped from the corner of the television onto the floor. My father coughed. Hit his chest with his palm like something was lodged in his throat. He put down his cigar and went to get water from the kitchen. I went to wipe the water off the screen. My sleeve stained with salt from the ocean, already beading back.

I sat down and stared at the screen, at the people seeking refuge. The angle of the light made their shadows stretch along bronze panels. Made them dark as that space in the wheel wells. Made something shaped like a Wolf appear on the walls. I stared at the shadow and saw yellow eyes again. Looking back at us. Counting all the bodies with wires inside them.

When my father returned, the reporter announced the doors to the dome had opened. People streamed into the ark. The screen clicked to vulture view. The city in aerial. The great gray ocean beyond it. The pain in my hips flared. I winced and pressed my palm into my back. My father coughed again and rubbed his knee. I saw a flash in his leg like something glinting beneath his skin. But it was gone as soon as he removed his hand. Just my father beside me. Just his city under siege. Just bodies seeking shelter in arks we prayed would be enough to stop the ocean.

THE STARVING ARK

I watched my father watch the storm the day it made landfall. He coughed and checked his watch. Glanced at the phone. Aligned the forecasts with New Orleans, an hour behind. As if an hour was enough to ensure everyone survived.

He called my uncle earlier that day. They talked for an hour. First about the storm, the latest predictions and paths. Then shifted to shared memories. The neighbors they played with. The bike they shared. Their grandmother's stories. The superstitions she whispered like she was offering them something on fire.

I could hear my uncle's voice faintly through the line. *It's getting dark. I better go. Love you bro.* My father placed the phone back on its cradle. Heavy as stone boxes that kept the dead from the ocean.

My father sank into the couch. Cleared his throat. Relayed the final preparations. Boarded windows and batteries. Branches shorn. Bathtubs filled. Our family wrapped in their house like a hymn. He stared at the ceiling and asked if he'd ever told me his grandmother's stories. The ones about the Wolf that stalked the shadows for broken Lent. The beast that would tear seven years of sacrilege from your throat.

I stared at the television. At aerial views of the ark. The crowds in the dome. Bags strung across their backs like wires. Supplies like surnames combined. Half-moon bruises under their eyes. New bodies to rewrite the map. The ocean pooling at the corner of the screen. The ocean dripping into our house. The ocean evaporating on the floor so we would breathe it into our lungs.

My father coughed. Struggled to dislodge something from his throat. I rubbed his back and told him no. I hadn't heard the stories. He smiled. Swallowed. Shook his head. Said his grandmother had always been eccentric and leaned back against the couch as water dripped from the screen and something burned in my hips.

He took the remote and raised the volume on the news. Returned to repeating the names of every memory he recognized. His vigil modeled on maps of storm paths and ark wrecks and wires on the ocean floor. The beginning of his childhood being erased.

I wanted to say something that would stop the storm. Stop the water beading into our house. Stop the waves from cresting the levees. Stop the ocean and its insatiable hunger. But there was miasma pooling at our feet, worlds away from the wreckage. And the wires in our bodies were flashing like a beacon for the brine to find us.

My father started coughing again and asked if I would get him more coffee. I went to the kitchen and pressed my hands into the counter. Something solid. Like the levees around the city. Like cemeteries and iron gates. Like there were names we could save from the jaws of the Atlantic. I pleaded with the ocean. *Please. This doesn't have to be a massacre. The dome doesn't have to become an ark. This storm doesn't have to be our inheritance coming to claim us.*

I poured his coffee and brought it to the living room. My father didn't look away from the screen. I placed his mug on the table and sipped my own. It tasted like copper in my mouth. I looked at the television. The ocean kept dripping from the screen. Kept suffusing our lungs. He never told me, but I knew those stories already. They were made of bloodlines and wires already in our bodies. Already binding us to tragedy. Hurricane-shaped and spiraling into a thousand arms the levees would either save or lead to slaughter.

MOONRISE OVER MIASMA

We kept vigil once Katrina began. Black coffee and white cigar smoke. My father cross-legged on the couch. Back hunched. Staring at the television. The storm reflecting on his glasses. The storm in his irises. The ocean dripping through the screen.

I was beginning to see glimpses of the Wolf everywhere. In corners behind anchors broadcasting updates before the blackouts descended. In the dark beneath the levees. In every shadow of the ark. Like it was trying to rewrite this genealogy of wires and waves.

The storm clawed through New Orleans in great black sheets. Redrew the city in dark water. The ocean threw itself against borderlands and shores. Against our salvaged names. Against the levees meant to keep our drowning at bay. An open mouth trying to swallow New Orleans whole.

Every update was bad or worse. Memories were erased. Estimates of the dead and the living they would leave behind. The water began dripping faster through the screen. My father coughed and wrapped his late mother's rosary around his hand. Clutched the cross so tight it pierced his palm.

The television cut to breaking news. My father winced and rubbed his knee. The wires hissed in my hips. The anchor onscreen began to repeat what we feared. The levees had been breached. The water was surging into the city. Cleaving channels through parish lines. Throwing itself against the bronze hull of the ark. Roaring toward homes. Gorging on wires. Dissolving plaster saints in the brine. Leaving trails pale as moonrise streaking toward the sea.

My father coughed. Tried to dislodge something from this throat. I rubbed his back and watched the water fall from the screen and spread on the floor. Spread into the room. Spread into our throats, empty of anything to say. Like the shore after the exile. Like a howl cloaked in thunder. Like lines of moonlight no one's left to see.

We watched the news in silence as New Orleans drowned. My father cradled the rosary in his hand. Crimson beads turned black in the darkness of his palm. I sat beside him, thinking about the names set for erasure. The stone boxes that couldn't save them. The wires we wouldn't discuss. The brine already in our mouths.

My father coughed again. I placed my hand on his knee and didn't say what the storm was doing or that the Wolf was watching us. That the ocean already had our scents. That the cells in our throats were suffused with the Atlantic and twisting into a map of dark and drowning waters.

IN BEDS MARKED FOR BURNING

We watched the aftermath like sentries. The city submerged. Reefs made of rosaries and ripped doors. The bronze ark surrounded by water named miasma. Telephone poles rising through the flood like masts.

The phone rang days later. My father braced the cradle. We heard his brother's voice. They were safe. The house intact. But the power lines were down. My uncle asked my father for the news they couldn't see. A name. A place. A memory. My father choked on the repetition of *gone*. His voice so strained it sounded like *run*.

He took the phone and left the room. His voice curled down the hall. I stared at the screen. At the ocean dripping from the corner. At the aerial footage of the ark. The survivors huddled inside. The survivors trapped in their homes. Bathtubs like cradles. Walls like rafts. The wreckage rearranging, teal to blue to black.

I got up to wipe the water off the screen. Off the floor where it pooled. To erase this tendril of the ocean seeping into our throats. But it wouldn't change that the city was still submerged. Every wire was tied to broken wood and starcharts. Tied to the names of all the missing. Their unheard prayers like artifacts we'd have to burn to stop the Atlantic from swallowing them.

My father came back to the living room. Said *I love you bro* as my uncle hung up to preserve the battery. The dial tone divided us. My father kept the phone pressed to his face. I wiped the rest of the water from the floor, took the phone from his hand, and placed it on the cradle. I wrapped my arms around him as if we could change what happened. As if I could grab a wire and make this go away.

He ran his hand over my hair then sat on the couch. Onscreen, the footage came faster. Flooded parishes. Bodies and homes. Walls made soft from the weight of the ocean. Its hunger refusing to ebb from New Orleans.

I looked at that water and wanted to scream *what's left for you to take?* The wires flared down my legs. I already knew the answer. I could already imagine some dark skate of water at night. A house and a boat poling toward it. The movement a mutation. Someone pushing cracked walls apart. The Wolf in the darkness, frozen. Consigned to shadow as copper flickered in the floodlights as hands pulled wires from the water. Created coils like nests. A pile growing in the aft. Like it was that easy to erase this history. Like drowning wasn't written on our cells. Like we could excise the wires from our bodies and make the ocean forget us.

My father fell asleep on the couch that night. His hand on his knee. I placed a blanket over him and kissed his forehead. He'd still wake up to this reality. To his childhood erased. To wreckage we'd have to burn if we wanted to survive the brine.

I turned off the living room lights. In the darkness, the television flooded the room with blue. The Atlantic seeped through the screen. It found us in that storm. Found my father and his throat. Began to turn his body into a map of the city submerged. A thousand spider arms. A thousand storms and all their spirals. A thousand wires we couldn't save.

The wires in my hips screamed. Burned down my legs. And something howled in the woods surrounding our house as the ocean settled against the ark, hundreds of miles away.

SARCOMA

WE BROKE LENT FOR SEVEN YEARS

We found the mass in my father's throat at the start of Lent. Two years after we sat like sentries as the storm consumed his city and the ocean dripped through the screen.

I noticed him eating less the month before. Eschewing solids. Coughing more. Clearing his throat as if he could exorcize the block. He said he was fine, but his grocery lists were made of liquids. New notches punched into his belt. The ocean encroaching on the house.

He drove himself to the hospital the day he couldn't swallow. The day water lodged in his throat like a levee blocked its path. He called me from the waiting room. *They're still running tests* he said. But we already knew the diagnosis. A tumor in his throat from where the ocean got in. Plain as families in the belly of the ark. Solid as cemetary boxes the storm washed away.

They kept him in the hospital overnight for observation. I paced the halls of our home. Our inheritance growing in his body like a family tree. I kicked the spot on the floor where the ocean dripped through the screen. The Atlantic sewed this agenda down his throat. Rewrote our history in cells like survivors clinging to the coast.

I walked to his bedroom, dark as drowning. As if I could find exactly where this began. Where the first levees broke. Where the architects sunk the arks and consigned white hands to brine. The taste of salt before the water surged. The boats sliding silent through the city. The wires pulled from waves. The wires in our bodies. The wires clinging to the mast. Copper coils that grew from a crossing centuries before. Everything angled down into the ocean.

I stood at the foot of his bed. Moonglow dripped like communion. Shadows cut across the room. I stared at the corner. At something darker coming into view. A shape from wheel wells and bronze walls. The Wolf seized in the shadows.

Rougarou. Born from drowning and broken Lent. Born from our failure to run. The beast blinked shadow to shadow. Corner to closet to bed. We'd fled, but the Wolf was always with us. Frozen save for its ability to witness and warn. It opened two yellow eyes. Stared back. And growled.

I tried to scream but the sound wrapped around my tongue like a wire. Like a massacre. Like a slaughter small enough to hold. The wires burning in my hips. Moonlight pouring in. Pointing down where the copper led. Down where this family's swept. Down and glinting where we're buried in the ocean.

Rougarou blinked to the corner then disappeared. I ran to the window and stared outside. There was nothing but bare hydrangea bushes and elms. I couldn't see it, but I knew the Wolf was there. Back-bent knees and yellow eyes. Metastasis tangled in its fangs.

I turned on all the lights in the house. Blocked the basement. Sat on the living room floor by the fireplace. Black fans of soot like coming waves.

I stared at the salt stain where the Atlantic dripped in. The Wolf was here now. But the scale in my father's neck had tipped long before. Seven years of Lent and levees. Of hulls and hymnals sung in darkness. In the drowning that was always our inheritance because someone had to carry the copper and all the tragedy it contains back to the ocean.

HIS THROAT BECAME A COASTLINE

All my father's appointments began with scans of his neck. White vertebrae against fluorescent screens. His esophagus stretched from the mass. The edges of the tumor blazing. A map stored in his cells.

The doctor handed us copies of the scans. I traced the tumor's outline. Caught the Wolf in the blackness outside his body.

My father's throat became a coastline. A map of forced migrations. Seaboard parallel to spine. The survivors scattered. The ocean aglow. Our cartography coming to a head. Rougarou snarled in the darker masses. We never survived the arks. We never survived all those times we didn't run.

The ocean pooled in my father's esophagus. Its waves were named miasma. Named hunger. Our family dragged from land to water. The Atlantic drowning him in slow motion. Clear as the tumor on the sheet.

The doctor explained the treatment. Chemo, radiation, surgery. Survive. *We caught this in time. We should be able to freeze the progression.* He said the treatments would harden the mass so they could cut this condition from his throat. Stretch his esophagus together. Sew. Like the massacre never happened. Like metastasis and migration can be ripped from the coast and disappear.

But the Wolf was always in the corners of those scans. Snarling at the tumor and the ocean that caused it. Howling for passenger lists and plaster saints. The bodies under black water. The wreckage collected over generations.

My father beamed with promises of a future where he could swallow. He smiled and shook the doctor's hand. Signed the waivers like this would be okay.

Waves filled my head. The wires burned down my hips. The scans kept shaking in my hands. Rougarou on every screen. Couldn't they see the masts in the distance? The cracks in the levees? The miasma dripping in? Like a cypher we'd understand later in spring. Like a reckoning waiting to happen on this new coastline drawn down my father's throat.

But my father smiled. Laughed with the doctor. Took prescriptions written on white leaves. Put on his coat and left for the car. I paused in the exam room. Rougarou snarled from under the table. The tumor flickered on the scans. Still growing in my father's neck. A map of all the times we didn't run from the masts. Of the copper wires gathered at last.

My father called from the hallway. Waved for me to follow.
My heels clicked on the tile. Wires smoldered in my hips. I
walked to his side so we could leave together. Our reckoning
was here. And we'd decided to defy the ocean to try and save
him.

THE WOLF IN THE WHEEL WELLS

We left the appointment in mid-winter dark. The doctor's plan to remove the tumor. Remission on our lips. But a different possibility was wrapped around our tongues. So we walked through the parking lot to the car in silence. The Wolf was waiting in the wheel wells when we arrived.

We unlocked the doors and secured the belts. The key trembled in my father's hand. He said that I'd have to learn to drive and something yellow flickered in the rotations as the wheels started spinning and the blinker signaled home.

My father drove. His skin hung from his starving frame. Red skies signaled snow. A coming storm made of manageable memories of drowning. Back roads like liturgies curved through the dark. I read through the prescriptions we'd been instructed to buy. Every errand an iteration of goodbye.

The doctors had a plan. But the signs curled like chokeweeds. Like the birches bending around us. Like the recipes he said he'd make once he could swallow. Like the Wolf wasn't with us in the car.

My father winced. Fingered the spot in his neck above the mass. The elms crossed their branches. Shadows against the sky. I traced chemo in the frost on the window and caught yellow eyes in the rearview mirror.

I stared at the Wolf and begged it to give me the cancer instead. Begged the beast to sand down my father's throat. Erase the coast. Scrawl the ocean somewhere in my body. I could be the birches curling like migrations. I could be the thing their branches spell. Ablaze with cells. Red like a coming storm. We couldn't cut the name from the coast and sew the ends together like the massacre never happened. But I would swallow the ocean for him. Turn my body into the wreckage map. Become our land, our sea, our driftwood and bronze that were once the arks. Torn apart.

Rougarou disappeared. No sound from the shadows. But every sign was arsenic. Every birch a coming condition. Every slip of red sky a prognosis. A tumor grew where the ocean scratched deep in his throat. I wanted the beast to move everything knotting in my father's body and put it into mine.

The Wolf was in the wheel wells of the car as we drove. My father's starving frame flickered in the street lights. The growth clicked in his neck. The branches spelled metastasis in the coming snow. Rougarou snarled from the tires as we turned toward the pharmacy. The trajectory of this disease traced on all surrounding systems.

We parked as the snow started falling. My father shivered. I told him I'd go in. I told him to wait in the car. Far away from winter and prescriptions. From the dark that was drowning cut by snow. As I got out, he brought up driving again. And in the shadow of the car, we let his words fall heavy to the floor.

MOURNING SHORE

The next two months were a flood. The doctors sewed a
chemo port into my father's chest. Aimed lasers at his neck.
Sutured a tube into his stomach and taught us to connect it to
a machine that dripped nutrition into his body. A substitute
for swallowing. An arsenal designed to harden the mass so
the scalpel could erase it.

We collapsed his life into the living room. The reinvention of
home for disease. The machines tethered to the walls. Wires
like spokes. My father draped on the sofa. Too weak to pull
his starving body upstairs.

I moved the television to a table at my father's feet. Piled
books by his shoulders. Moved him to the chair to change
the sheets, white as the mornings the masts appeared. As the
storm gathered off the coast. As cancer became the ocean and
my father clung to shore.

The feeding machine demanded constant care. Refills and cleanings. The tubes always got blocked. Every error broadcast an alarm. Sirens that signaled he was starving. My father couldn't hear the tones. So I learned to sleep in shifts until the sound appeared. Tread downstairs to the living room. Fumbled to undo the block. To keep the machine running. To keep his drowning at bay.

I named the tubes *colony*, *parish*, and *home*. I strung hosanna in the curtains while he slept. I laid blankets over his body. I severed symbols of the ocean as if rituals could change the water's course.

We built barricades to block the Atlantic and filled his days with movies and spy novels. My father clipped recipes from magazines. Piled them beside him as if he could swallow the images. The feeding machine dripped like a metronome. But my father grew weaker. His skin turned white as sails. We lied about the implications and said this was temporary. As if cancer could be confined to a room. As if we could stay on this shore and not get dragged into the ocean.

Rougarou watched from behind the machines. Blinked to the corner where the Atlantic rode the wires through the screen and dripped onto the floor. The Wolf's presence a question as constant as the alarms. Can you confine this to a room? Can you refuse your inheritance? Can you be the seawall stopping every flood, alone?

The feeding machine alarms started again. The Wolf growled from the corner. I looked at my father, sound asleep. My father clinging to the shore. My father emaciated under blankets piled like waves. The ark sinking into the water.

I untangled the tubes and poured more nutrition in. I waited until the alarms stopped then went outside. I stood before the snow. Obliterating white. The woods arched toward the house that had become only this room. Only yellow eyes underfoot. Only the masts appearing on the horizon. Sailing for my father's neck.

We collapsed his life into that room and pretended there was no house. Pretended that the blankets were wool instead of waves. That he wasn't losing weight. That the mass was shrinking. That we were still on land. That the alarms weren't announcing his drowning.

THE STARVING ARK

We arrived at the hospital for his radiation one day in May. The first balm of spring. My father worn from months of feeding machines. From chemotherapy and starvation. He shivered under his sweater. His father's ring was loose on his finger. Violet bloomed beneath his skin.

The intake was always the same. His vitals were taken like clockwork. Blood pressure, temperature, weight. And wait. The nurse smiled and left the room. We sat in silence. My father on the examination table, haloed by fluorescent lights. Rougarou in the shadows beneath my chair.

The nurse returned. Explained my father had a fever. They'd admit him for observation to make sure it passed and resume the radiation once he was well. She said the treatments had weakened him, but this was common. She saw it all the time. *He'll be fine.*

He signed the papers and they wheeled him away. Led me to another room to wait until he was settled. Until he could tell me the things he wanted me to bring him. Until I could go back to that house, empty save for Rougarou and the ocean, encroaching.

My father's fever worsened. His delirium grew by the day. He turned books in his hands and cackled at covers he couldn't read. He tried to call his dead mother from the hospital phone. I pleaded with the nurses. *He's getting worse.* Every time, they told me this was normal and the Wolf growled from beneath the bed.

The next day, his bloodwork broke alarms. The doctor pulled me into the hall. They explained that there was scar tissue in his stomach where they sewed the feeding tube. That his intestines had knotted around it, blocking all the toxins from leaving his body.

They called it sepsis. I called it miasma. A new ocean lodged in the hold of my father's stomach like an ark.

The doctors explained the surgery. The urgency. The Wolf in their shadows. They said they had to operate today. I signed the forms and watched them swarm his room.

They let me say goodbye to my father on the gurney. He gave me his father's ring and told me he'd be back before he disappeared through doors that moved like a mouth.

I wrapped my father's sweater around my shoulders and sat in the waiting room. Another ark. Another dome. Another iteration of this family's stillness. The television hummed like nothing had changed. Like two rooms away, my father wasn't open on a table. Doctors untwisting his intestines like drowning could be rewound.

Strangers waited in that same silence. Rougarou blinked beneath their chairs. Everyone oblivious to the Wolf at their feet. I piled magazines to my lap for the weight. Rougarou in the dark between the pages. Wait. The growl. The arks cutting down the coast. The waves we named miasma. The drowned and their forgotten names.

For hours, I tried to imagine a better outcome into existence. That the doctors stared into my father's open stomach. That they found a wire and removed it. That they pulled so hard it dragged the arks ashore and severed us from the Atlantic. But waiting was my only recourse. And it could never keep the ocean away.

The Wolf blinked to the folds of my father's sweater as the nurse called my name. I followed her outside. She explained it went fine. He survived. But he was still under anesthesia. *So we wait. When he wakes up, he'll be okay.*

They moved him to the ICU. Wires on the walls. Tubes radiating from his body. Machines tracking every function on screens dark as drowning. I stayed. Watched and waited. A sentry on the shore. Rougarou in the shadows. I pulled my father's sweater tighter around my shoulders so we could scan the horizon together.

Hours later, the nurses urged me to leave. My father was still asleep. I couldn't ask if we'd saved him. Undone one massacure and pulled this ark ashore. Laid the boat on sheets white as sails and opened the hold so everyone could run.

Instead, I kissed his forehead. I told him I'd be back in the morning. And I left for that house dark as drowning with the Wolf curled in the folds of his sweater.

MOONRISE OVER MIASMA

Two weeks after the operation, my father still wasn't awake.
Each test was inconclusive, except the ones that were bad.
The sepsis wrecked his liver. His kidneys were so weak he
needed dialysis. His blood pressure fell steadily as snow.
They filled him with fluids to keep the volume high. All
that water weakened his skin. They told me I couldn't touch
him in one place too long or his flesh would slough from
his body.

I spent my days at his bedside. The Wolf snarled behind the
machines. I wore my father's sweater as if it could change
the trajectory of the text. I read to him until visiting hours
ended and the nurses led me out of his room into the night
with Rougarou in every shadow.

On Mother's Day of that impossible spring, I arrived to keep
the vigil. Saplings fanned against the brick. The hospital's

glass doors opened like a notch in the hull. I entered and the nurses grabbed my arms. Explained they were just about to call. That his blood pressure was dropping fast. That they'd pushed the maximum amount of fluids into his body. That there was nothing else they could do.

I wanted to run. Snap my knees backwards. Find the wires before they were packed into the dome. Before they were shoved onto boats. Burn the map of all the wrecks in the Atlantic. The nurses gripped tighter and led me to his room. Rougarou at my heels. The Wolf seething as the moon climbed to breach the horizon.

My father held an ocean in his body. His bed an altar for the ark. They warned me again not to touch him too much. His skin could still slough beneath my fingers. I held my hand above his arm and traced one finger down his wrist to make a furrow like a wire, blinding white.

Rougarou blinked to the undercarriage of the bed and growled. The ocean was here. Spilling into the room. Swelling to reclaim the drowning we'd tried to deny it. Eroding the coastline of his throat. Rearranging his body into all the massacres that came before.

Spring turned to night. The ocean rose to our knees. The machines wouldn't protect him much longer. I held his hand and traced bright lines down his arms until they glowed to break the waves. Disarm the drowning and the arks. The bodies and the boats. The coast. The times we could have run but never did.

The machines raged louder. The ocean rose to our waists. I slid my arms underneath my father's back and cradled him. As if I could lift him from the water in the room that was already in his body. The water that held the night the architects sunk the ark and the Atlantic swallowed his city whole.

I lifted him higher. His skin glowed white. The Wolf blinked beneath his spine. The brine. The machines screaming he was dying.

The ocean rose to my chest. My arms shaking with moonrise weight. I put my head to my father's ear and kept trying to scream run. But all that came out was *I love you.*

My father seized. His back arched. His body shot out of my arms. He breathed open-mouthed over the vent. Flashed back long enough to see the waves. Long enough to rise above the water. Long enough to run.

He dropped back into my arms. The nurses turned off the machines. The ocean ebbed from the room, denied.

He died. But he managed to escape his drowning.

A howl cut the hospital. His body in my arms. The Wolf between the bed and machines. One vein in my father's knee still glowing. A wire brighter than death. The one that ran from a hospital bed, from an ark, from the ocean. A wire I could see disappearing into the dark, leaving me alone on the shore with all the mourning that follows.

IN BEDS MARKED FOR BURNING

I sat with my father's body until I was sure he'd run as far as he could. I signed paperwork for cremation and the return of his effects. I kissed his cheek and left his body tagged for burning on the bed. An offering on an altar the Atlantic couldn't reach.

I left his room. The ICU. A recession of disinfectants. A comet through hospital halls. A copper trail behind me. The lobby where the nurses slung silence at my feet. High hosanna angled like the arc of his spine.

I stopped at the main entrance. Bleach on my breath. A chokehold of thunderheads outside. Lightning the color of his skin. I wanted the parking lot to be on fire. Everything ablaze. All the saplings curled to ash. All the roots erased. A multiplying weight. A pyroclasm to poison the ocean into forgetting we exist.

I stepped outside where nothing was burning. No trunks becoming charcoal. No wires becoming home. The impossibility calcified like the silence after the howl.

I walked across the parking lot to the car. Moonlit asphalt. Mica seized in the pavement. Saplings bent to the curb. Rougarou in the shadows. Yellow eyes charting the space between black planes and bloodlines. Parsing the present in moonglow like the depressions I left on my father's arms.

I stopped in the shadow between the lights. The Wolf blinked behind me. An injury in its fangs. Metastasis on its breath. A horizon along my collarbone where the ocean collapsed into graves. Where another moon would rise. Another ark would be swallowed. Another city would be submerged. Another person carrying a wire would be dragged beneath the sea because of all the copper woven into our bodies.

The Wolf blinked behind my neck. A warning. A cartography it couldn't stop. This was my inheritance. The copper burned through my hips. Every step thereafter would be fodder for the ocean. Our family had been marked for centuries. And after us, new generations of wires would be born and would drown in the black depths of the Atlantic.

The Wolf blinked away from parking lot shadows. Left me holding an abyss. Left me staring at the moon like an answer would drip silver through the dark. Left me rebraiding Acadia in every step as I walked away from the hospital. Away from my father. Away from the tumor that grew where the ocean eroded his throat.

Rougarou disappeared to where other wires were still sinking.

Blinked to where the water was mapping new spirals into open mouths. To where our family was wound in a coil of copper deep beneath the sea. But I could see it all like a map. Like the coast in vulture view. Like a lattice of wires stretching from shore to sea.

That night gave me my inheritance entire. It slipped silver through the dark and landed at my feet in the impossible stillness thereafter. The tumors and the arks. The arc of the Atlantic over the levees. The Wolf and the wires and the crossing that came before.

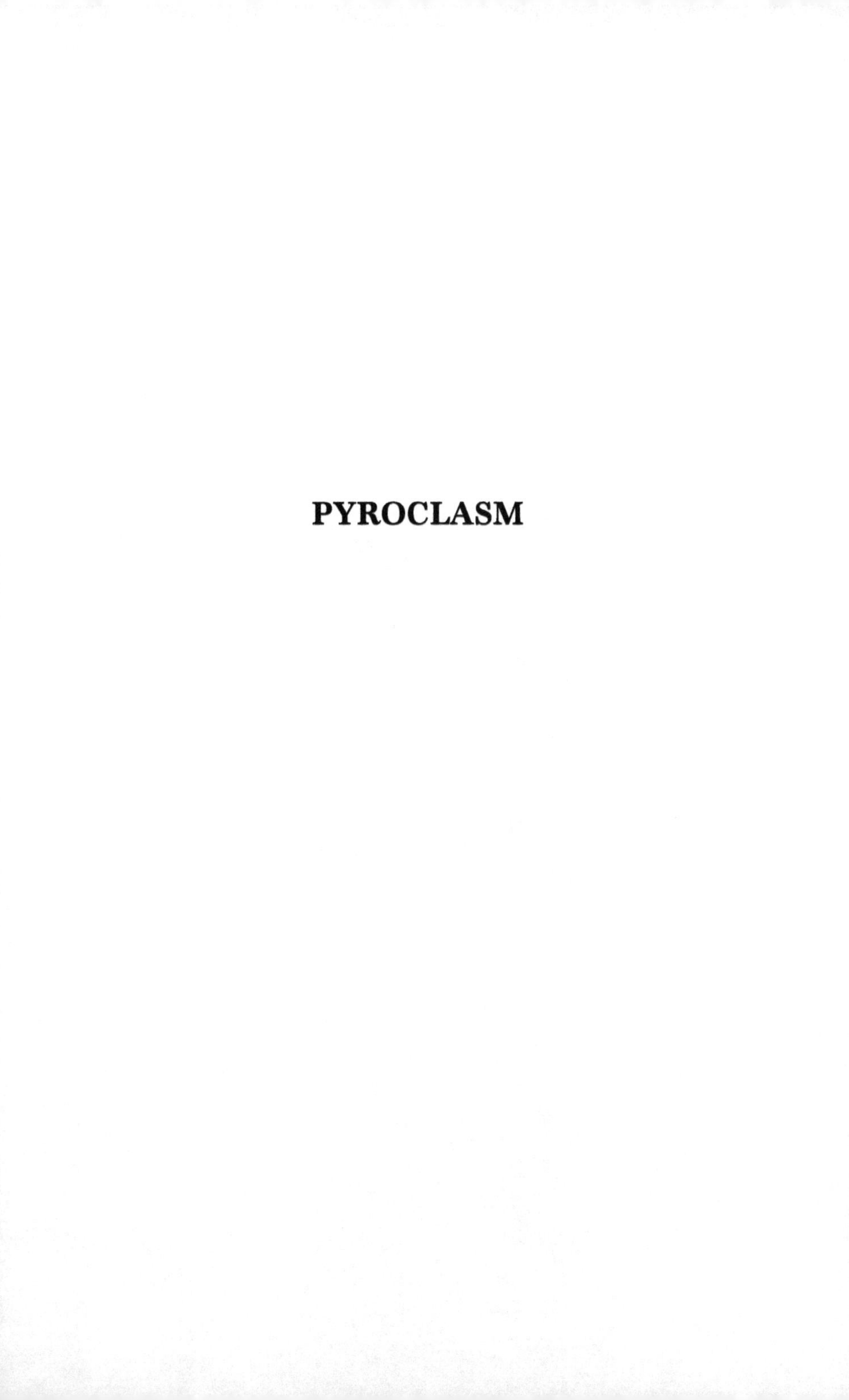

PYROCLASM

After my father's funeral, I sat in the living room. Surrounded by the books we piled by the couch. Surrounded by silence the alarms used to occupy. Surrounded by the Atlantic churning in my head.

I felt the ocean at his funeral. Circling the church. Seeping through foundation cracks. Marking my uncle as he flew home with half my father's ashes. A glint of copper in his neck. The wires stretched and gleaming. The waves we couldn't escape no matter what we tried.

I packed my father's books into empty boxes. My back to the couch, to the curtains, to the shadows and the Wolf's yellow eyes. Rougarou couldn't move, couldn't run, couldn't stop the ocean from swallowing the wires. Instead, it got dragged shadow to shadow. Drowning to drowning. Howling for every artifact the Atlantic claimed.

What did we really save the night my father ran? The living room still smelled like brine. The city was still waiting for the sea to surge over its spine. The arks were still in pieces at the bottom of the ocean. The colony eroded to white bones. Wires flashing beneath the black. The ocean was still in my head, my hips, my uncle's neck. Still in the graves waiting for us on the floor of the Atlantic. There would always be more. Another morning. Another storm. Another glint beneath our skin that would tell the water where to go.

The Atlantic churned louder in my head. Every noise cracked my skull. Rougarou snarled from the shadows behind me. I threw a book into the fireplace to stop the sounds. Its pages fanned like the ribs of a ship.

I glared. That first boat that cut the Atlantic in two. That first ark that set everything in motion. *You just had to cross the ocean. Ignite an inheritance that keeps coming to claim us.* I grabbed the matches off the mantle. Struck. Watched the sulfur flicker blue. Threw it on the book. The pages curled as they caught. The ark constricting. The city disappearing. A child becoming too small for her father to die.

I reached into the box. Grabbed a book. Threw it on the fire. Rougarou growled. The Atlantic hissed. I grabbed another book and threw. Watched them burn. The Wolf snarling behind me. The ocean roaring in my head. I wanted to send this inheritance back. Back before the cells, back before the storm, back before the sinking. Back to where it all began.

I grabbed books with each hand. The pages smelled like cancer. I threw them into the flames. I reached deeper into the box and felt his sweater. Promises the chemo couldn't keep. Threw it in and watched it catch. I grabbed the tubes from his feeding machine and hurled them into the fire.

　　　　　MEGHAN S. GUIDRY

The Atlantic in my skull. Waves breaking on bone. I watched everything burn and mouthed *run* as the flames carried them from the ocean.

I reached deeper in the box. Pulled out things I never packed. Photos dripping with storm surge. Cracked plaster saints, their moonrise eyes eroded flat. I told them to run and threw them in. I reached and felt something wrap around my wrists. Copper wires wrapped around my hands. I pulled out posters of everyone missing in the floods. It doesn't matter. We have to run.

I threw the posters in. Kept grabbing things from the box. New wires coiled up my forearms. I pulled faded fabric squares the colony used to pack their possessions and hurled them into the fire. The wires climbing higher. I pulled out sermons that couldn't save us. And weatherworn boards from where the ocean broke the ark.

The Wolf whimpered. Blinked to the shadow behind me. The ocean trying to crack my skull. The wires winding tighter. Cutting my arms. Tearing my hands. Tethered to something heavy at the bottom of the box. I wrapped my hands around it and ripped it out. A crack like thunder and breaking hulls.

I was holding the cross. Half copper. Half drowning green. The colony in my hands. On land. The pillar of flame. I threw the cross and all the wires into the fire. Started screaming *run* over the ocean. The cross turned blazing white and Rougarou howled as the fire swelled and burst and everything went silent and black as drowning.

I woke up the next morning. Ash covered the living room.

The front door was open. Spring light poured in. I pushed myself off the floor. Checked my arms. No marks from where the wires cut. No bottomless box. Nothing left in the fireplace.

I stood and looked down. Saw depressions in the soot that led to the door. Massive black prints on the stoop that disappeared into the forest surrounding the house.

There was another set of tracks starting from where my shadow had been cast the night before. They were less sure. Like something unsteady had first dragged itself on its knees. I followed them to the fireplace, caked in soot save for one disrupted line. I brushed the ashes away. Then I saw it. Deep gouges in the stone. Claw marks making letters. A message in new movement's shaking hand. An anagram of run and goodbye.

Blessed was the beast who found the wires
and pulled us safe ashore.

ACKNOWLEDGMENTS

In 2011, four years after losing my father, I wanted to write a book about him, about missing someone so much it felt like drowning. I began sketching short sections about the days in the hospital leading to his death—moments that felt and still feel impossible. At the time I started writing what would become *Kinesiophobia* I was still too wounded, too deep in the raw immediacy of grief to get very far in the writing.

Over the next 8 years, I tried over and over to return to this book. Nothing ever worked. Nothing I added felt like it fit. I tried to edit what I had already written and revised myself in circles. But there was one line from those first sketches that survived, impossibly untouched, and lives in the book you're holding now.

I wanted the parking lot to be on fire.

This line is in reference to the moment about an hour after my father died, after I'd signed all the post-death paperwork and gotten his clothes handed to me in a neon pink plastic bag labeled "patient effects." I moved through those steps on auto-pilot, making it as far as the hospital's main entrance before it hit me. I wanted the parking lot to be on fire.

I wanted smoke and flames and ash I wanted the visible, physical world to mirror what happened. To acknowledge it. I wanted some sign that what had just happened was as apocalyptic as it felt. I wanted something to affirm the unfairness and impossibility of one simple fact: my father was dead and I wasn't.

The parking lot was fine and I became furious. Like the unchanged nature of the outside was an erasure of what had just happened.

That's why that line survived. It knew something about the nature of this book long before I did. *Kinesiophobia* was never meant to be a literal recounting of the events that led to my father's death. It was meant to be mythology of how we arrived at that point, a seismic reimagining of family history, a testament to how the raw immediacy of trauma and grief feel.

It's a story of my father's family history and 400 years of the tragedy inaction brings. It's a story of how trauma flows through generations, embedding itself like a wire. It's a story of a Wolf braided into my family's history and a sentient ocean coming to claim us. It's a story about how trauma turns to myth over time, and what happens when we the living inherit that mythology from the dead.

Most importantly, it's the book I wish I'd had the night my father died, and all the nights that have come after.

I am immensely grateful to so many people for their support of this book in its long journey to become real, and their support of me in every way possible.

I want to start by first thanking the Thera Books team for selecting this work, for publishing it, and for your unwavering belief in this book and in me: Donnelle McGee (publisher), Nia McGee (copy editor), Colleen Mills (assistant editor), Mona Z. Kraculdy (cover design), Jenna Sumpter (copy editor), and Carla Baja (book design and marketing).

My deepest thanks to artist Dawn Baja for her work creating a cover more haunting and beautiful than I could even have imagined.

I am forever grateful to my family, especially Pert and Betty Guidry and Joe and Donna Lembo, for your support throughout that time, for sitting with me and Louis in the hospital as he passed from this world to the next, and for the love and joy you bring to me today.

To Coleman McNear: you sat with me and my father during that awful time. I can't imagine a world without our friendship, our unwavering bond, and our capacity to laugh even in the darkest situations.

Dearest Rachel Pollack, none of this would be possible without you, without the wisdom and guidance and friendship you showed me as my writing teacher, mentor, and friend. That you saw me as a writer from the moment we met remains the honor of a lifetime. I treasure those words, and will spend the rest of my life trying to live up to them.

Radiant Jeanne Mackin, you met me as a new advisee six weeks after my father died, and without hesitation you wrapped me in more care, support, and encouragement than I could have imagined. You made me a better writer and a more compassionate person through your pesence in my life.

None of this would be possible without the lifelong support of the incredible teachers I've been lucky to learn from: Amy Hollywood, Michael D. Jackson, David Lamberth, Mary Kay Mahoney, Michael Motia, Kevin Plunkett, Steven Schewartzky, and Paul Vatalaro. Something each of you taught me has found a home in this book. I am forever grateful for your wisdom and mentorship.

For Lindsey Rogers, whose coaching in 2019 helped me find my way back to myself and, through that, find my way back to this book after I had all but given up.

I am grateful to the journals, editors, conductors, and ensembles that have published both excerpts of this book and my other strange writings about grief and love: *34 Orchard* (editor Kristi Petersen Schoonover), *Applied Sentience* (editors Esther Boyd & Paul Chiarello), *The Grey Alley Anthologies* at Empty City Press (ed. Keith Backhaus), the Handel Society of Dartmouth College, the *Harvard Divinity Bulletin* (editor Wendy McDowell and guest editor Ingrid Norton), the Ithaca College Choir and Symphony Orchestra, and Juventas New Music Ensemble (artistic directors Lydia Yankovskaya and Oliver Caplan).

I remain forever grateful to the friends who never stopped encouraging me to write this book, and who reminded me I was a writer even when I didn't believe them: Keith Backhaus, Minda Berbecco, Michael Berkowitz, Oliver Caplan, C.D. Collins, Chad Dean, Will Fertman, Debbie Finkelstein, Meg Fuchs, Joe Gualtieri, Afroza Hossain, Jason Leary, Eugénie Olson, Giselle Ferro Puigbo, Kristi Petersen Schoonover, Elise Scott, Lisa Vaas, Christopher Wilson, and Marc Zeagans. Thank you for seeing me when I couldn't see myself.

My sincerest thanks to those friends who held me in joy in the darkest periods of creating this work—even if you didn't know it, you were keeping my head above water: Sheena Anello, Chris Beagan (and Mortimer), Pearl Brault, Sandra Canas, Mitul Daiyan, Ryan DePalma, Katie DesBois, Natalie Diffloth, Abbie Dusseldorp, Isadel Eddy, Jenna Funsten, Michael Grady, Dan Hall, Lauren Hall, Maleha Haroon, Rakesh Kheterpal, Mike Leonard, Liaise Lima, Amy Litrenta, Ben Mansour, Rosanna Salgado McDonald, Sheila Mousavi, Aziza Musa, Jenna Nimar, Jason Pavel, Azael Paz, Chris Petre-Baumer, Rena Sokolow, Daron Sharps, James Vamboi, and Brian Ward.

Lastly, I want to thank my dad, Louis Guidry, for the 23 years we had together. No amount of time was ever going to be enough to spend with you, but I will always be grateful for the time we had. And I am immensely proud to this day to be your daughter.

ABOUT THE AUTHOR

Meghan Guidry works across genres by fusing poetry, memoir, and magical realism to highlight emotional truths and inner landscapes. Central to her work is the exploration of grief—how it manifests in memory and ritual, and the mythologies we create to live alongside loss.

Meghan's work has appeared in the *34 Orchard, Harvard Divinity Bulletin, Applied Sentience,* and *The Grey Alley* from Empty City Press. She is the creator of *No New Mythology,* a monthly literary series that explores trauma, grief, and healing through the lens of classical mythology. Meghan also collaborates with composers on choral lyrics and libretto for new operas.

Meghan lives in Boston with her cat Sam. When she's not writing, you can find her swimming, playing RPGs, and on a quest to find the best chocolate in the world. Learn more, stay in touch, and send chocolate recommendations at meghansguidry.com.

ABOUT THE PRESS

Thera Books is an independent publishing house uplifting the voices of writers across all intersections. Based in Sacramento, California, we aim to publish writers pushing the boundaries of literature and writing about what it means to be human.

www.thetherabooks.com

www.ingramcontent.com/pod-product-compliance
Lightning Source LLC
Chambersburg PA
CBHW031548310726
48971CB00008B/2677